Ladybird, Ladybird

For my sister, Sylvia

Copyright ©1988 by Ruth Brown.

The rights of Ruth Brown to be identified as the author and illustrator of this work have been asserted by her in accordance with the Copyright, Designs and Patents Act, 1988.

First published in Great Britain in 1988 by Andersen Press Ltd. 20 Vauxhall Bridge Road, London SW1V 2SA.

Published in Australia by Random House Australia Pty., 20 Alfred Street, Milsons Point, Sydney, NSW 2061.

This paperback edition first published in 2001 by Andersen Press Ltd.

All rights reserved. Colour separated in Switzerland by Photolitho AG, Zürich.

Printed and bound in Italy by Grafiche AZ, Verona.

10 9 8 7 6 5 4 3 2

British Library Cataloguing in Publication Data available.

ISBN 1 84270 040 5

This book has been printed on acid-free paper

Ladybird, Ladybird
Ruth Brown

Andersen Press · London

Ladybird, Ladybird, fly away home,
Your house is on fire, your children are gone.

Ladybird, Ladybird, blown by the breeze,
Over the cornfields, and over the trees.

Ladybird, Ladybird, lands in some smoke.
There's really a fire; it wasn't a joke.

Ladybird, Ladybird, fly away, fly.
That frog has a hungry look in his eye.

Ladybird, Ladybird, which way to go?
The old snail is friendly, but he doesn't know.

Ladybird, Ladybird, please do not pause
Close to those dangerous, razor-sharp claws.

Ladybird, Ladybird, pass the pig by.
He's too full to think: too lazy to try.

Ladybird, Ladybird, go to the crow.
Ask him the way home, he'll probably know.

Ladybird, Ladybird, lost in the wood.
Squirrel can't help, though she wishes she could.

Ladybird, Ladybird, will she be blown
Further away from her children and home?

Ladybird, Ladybird, help is at hand.
The bees will show you the lie of the land.

Ladybird, Ladybird, all's clear at last.
Fly to your children, fly home to them fast.

Ladybird, Ladybird, safely back home.
It isn't on fire, and your children aren't gone.

They are all sound asleep, snug in their nest.
Now you can join them; at last you can rest.

More Andersen Press paperback picture books!